TBH, You Know What I Mean

Also by Lisa Greenwald

The Friendship List Series
11 Before 12
12 Before 13
13 and Counting

The TBH Series
TBH, This Is SO Awkward
TBH, This May Be TMI
TBH, Too Much Drama
TBH, IDK What's Next

TBH, You Know What I Mean

KATHERINE TEGEN BOOKS
An Imprint of HarperCollins Publishers

BY LISA GREENWALD
Author of the Friendship List series

Katherine Tegen Books is an imprint of HarperCollins Publishers.

TBH #6: TBH, You Know What I Mean
Copyright © 2020 by Lisa Greenwald
Emoji icons provided by EmojiOne

ISBN 978-0-06-290624-3 (hardback)
ISBN 978-0-06-299662-6 (pbk.)

Typography by Molly Fehr
21 22 23 24 25   PC/LSCC   11 10 9 8 7 6 5 4 3 2 1
❖
First Edition

For Rhonda,
unofficial publicist extraordinaire

Vishal, Prianka

VISHAL

Yo

PRIANKA

What's up

VISHAL

Did you do this women's history month essay

PRIANKA

Yeah working on it now

Writing about my aunties

VISHAL

Ughhhhhhh

PRIANKA

What?

1

VISHAL

Why do we need to do another essay

PRIANKA

It's important to celebrate women, Vishal

VISHAL

What about celebrating men

PRIANKA

I cannot believe u just said that

VISHAL

What's the big deal

PRIANKA

It's women's history month

VISHAL

I know

What about men's history month

PRIANKA

Are you serious rn ???

2

VISHAL

What

PRIANKA

Duh every month is men's history month

Don't you see that

VISHAL

Ummm not really

Sorry to offend tho

PRIANKA

Also, um, what's the deal w/ #broboom

VISHAL

It's just a thing people are saying IDK

Like the guys in school teaming up

PRIANKA

For what tho

VISHAL

Just bc like in the news lately it's all the women's stuff going on so we wanted our own thing

PRIANKA

Who made that up

VISHAL

No clue

PRIANKA

But don't u see all of life is a boys + men's thing since basically the beginning of time?

VISHAL

Huh?

PRIANKA

Men don't need to be celebrated or highlighted bc they always had the rights—to vote, to work outside the home, to go to school, a million things

Women have always had to struggle

VISHAL

R u really mad

PRIANKA

It's a little shocking u need
me 2 point this out to u

VISHAL

Um ok

Again sorry to offend

PRIANKA

K I got that

VISHAL

Hahahahahahahah

Good talk

PRIANKA

Yeah but I gotta run

VISHAL

K

PRIANKA

Talk later bye

BOYS ARE SO CLUELESS

PRIANKA

Omg u guys

Why are boys soooooo out of it ??

GABRIELLE

??

PRIANKA

Vishal does not get why it's dumb to suggest there should be a men's history month 😐 😐 😐

6

GABRIELLE

LOL

PRIANKA

And he was whining about the assignment

GABRIELLE

Was he joking

PRIANKA

Kinda but not totally

Funny but not funny ya know

CECILY

Ya

They need to be enlightened

We need to help them 🤭🤭🤭

VICTORIA

Hahahaha 😛😛

PRIANKA

Seriously

PRIANKA

They just don't really have a sense of the around them

GABRIELLE

I guess

IDK

CECILY

This doesn't make u guys so mad ⁉️‼️

PRIANKA

It does❗

VICTORIA

I don't pay attention that much TBH

GABRIELLE

Same

Too much going on 😑😑🙀

Prianka, Cecily

PRIANKA

Cece?

CECILY

Ya

PRIANKA

I feel like u r the only one who gets what I was saying about boys 😣😣

CECILY

Oh haha IDK

PRIANKA

No I mean it

CECILY

I know what u r saying

We are the deep thinkers in the group

9

CECILY

Don't tell the others tho

Actually we are side chatting now

We should stop

PRIANKA

True ok 🖤🖤

Bye ✌️✌️

CECILY

Mwah 😘

Love you, Pri

Prianka's Poetry Journal

Sometimes I wish
I went to an all-girls school
It would be so civilized
No roughhousing in the hallway
No dumb comments
Well maybe some
But not as many
Boys are great
But they can also be so dumb
When do they grow up
I wish I knew

Cecily, Gabrielle

GABRIELLE

Cece?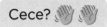

CECILY

Hi

GABRIELLE

Are u around this week after school

HW is sooooo hard & I thought maybe u could help me 🙏🙌🙇

CECILY

I think I'm around yeah

Just text me the morning u want to meet, k?

GABRIELLE

K

GABRIELLE

Thank u SOO much 🙌 🙌 🙌

CECILY

Mwah 😘 😘 😘 😘 😘

From: Jeremy Cavanaugh
To: Anthony Mawslin
Subject: RE: DUDE!

Ugghhhhhh meant to forward to u...

> **From:** Anthony Mawslin
> **To:** Jeremy Cavanaugh
> **Subject:** DUDE
>
> Why did you just reply all to that email????
>
> > **From:** Jeremy Cavanaugh
> > **To:** Honors History Section 2
> > **Subject:** RE: Women's History Month assignment
> >
> > Ugggghhhhhhh. #broboom
> >
> > ———————————————————————————
> >
> > **From:** Rose Summer
> > **To:** Honors History Section 2
> > **Subject:** Women's History Month assignment

14

Hello, students:

I wanted to email in case you forget to check your Student Portal Notes. Please be prepared to share your Women's History Month assignment with the class. I want to work on our public speaking. I'll bring in treats for us all to share.

Happy writing!
Ms. Summer

It isn't enough to talk about peace. One must believe in it. And it isn't enough to believe in it. One must work at it. —*Eleanor Roosevelt*

Dear Ms. Summer:

We're not allowed to use laptops in study hall today due to some kids violating the computer policy, so I'm leaving you a note. What Jeremy Cavanaugh wrote was not acceptable. This "bro boom" thing is out of hand. Boys are saying it all the time now. I can't sit by and let things like this go unnoticed. These little things add up to be big things. I hope we can discuss this further.

Thank you,
Cecily Anderson

BOYS ARE SO CLUELESS

C P G V

Hi

Anyone still up

I have to tell u about the email Jeremy accidentally sent to our whole history class

I can't sleep

He is so rude

GABRIELLE

Crying over hw

What's up

CECILY

Just soooooo mad @ Jeremy

GABRIELLE

Cavanaugh or Sulren?

CECILY

Cav

He wrote ughhhhhh about us all sharing our women's history month assignments and used that dumb broboom hashtag

He sent it to the whole class and Ms. Summer was on the email

PRIANKA

Vishal says that all the time

CECILY

OMG that is nuts

VICTORIA

Really really nuts

GABRIELLE

Now that I think about it the boys in my gym class are always yelling out broboom like doofuses

VICTORIA

Yeah I hear boys say it all the time in the hall 😖

What does it even mean

PRIANKA

Something about boys standing out since there's so much about women in the news lately 😖🙍🙍🙍

Boys teaming up or something

CECILY

Ewwwww 😤 😤

GABRIELLE

For real

That is not cool

CECILY

Ugh I am so mad

I wrote to Ms. Summer about Jeremy's email

She saw it but I had to say something anyway

Us girls have to stand up for ourselves

We need to take a stand !!!

And not allow this to go on 🙈🙈

GABRIELLE

Def ☝️☝️

Go, Cece 👊👊

K back 2 work for me 👋👋

CECILY

❤️❤️❤️

Dear Victoria,

We found this at that cute artsy store downtown and knew you'd love it! How are you?

We miss you in Philly!!! Come visit soon, pleaaasseeeee.

xoxoxox Kim & Nic

PS Pick out a postcard and send one back to us, okay?

Will be fun! We can be POSTCARD PALS! LOL :)

PPS POSTCARD PALS

FOR LIFE

To: V

131š

Yorkv

Miriam, Gabrielle

MIRIAM

R u coming over after school ??

GABRIELLE

Yeah

MIRIAM

Cool so excited 🎉 🎉 🎉

GABRIELLE

Same

Need to do hw tho

Drowning

MIRIAM

OMG why ????

GABRIELLE

It is sooo hard for me

Not for u?

Not really 🙄🙄

Hmmm ok

Maybe u can help me

Sure

ICB Sami is @ private school 😲😲

Me neither

I wonder if it's easier or harder than our school

She is in serious trouble, though

MIRIAM

No phone for a year

And she's in therapy to figure stuff out

Her parents felt like she needed a smaller school environment

Kind of amazing she got in tho since she was expelled from here

GABRIELLE

Yeah that's true

Hmmm maybe smaller environ will help her IDK 🤔🤔🤔

Hope she sorts out her issues & doesn't feel the need to rank the kids @ her new school 😬😬😬

R u upset she's not here anymore

MIRIAM

A little

MIRIAM

Eloise is crushed 😭😭😭

She wants 2 go with her

GABRIELLE

Will she

MIRIAM

IDK pos

Eloise gets whatever she wants pretty much 😵😵

TBH I feel like so many people here r like that

YKWIM?

GABRIELLE

Yeah I def do

I gtg now

So sorry

Almost got caught messaging in study hall againnnnnn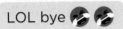

MIRIAM

LOL bye 😭😭

From: Cecily Anderson
To: Mr. Akiyama
Subject: International Women's Day

Dear Mr. Akiyama:

I know this is very short notice because International Women's Day is only a few days away. It's actually on a Sunday so that makes this even trickier, but I think we need to have an event for it at school. I'm sort of surprised we haven't had one before.

Can we make this happen on Friday? We can highlight amazing women in history and in our community: everyone from the teachers to the cafeteria staff to the people in the main office. We need to highlight all women and celebrate them and get everyone involved! This is very important in light of some recent events. Ask Ms. Summer if you're curious. She is doing a special thing for Women's History Month in class, but I think we can actually make it a whole-day, school-wide event.

I'm happy to come speak to you in person as well.

Please say yes.

Thank you,
Cecily Anderson

I'm not afraid of storms, for I'm learning how to sail my ship.
—Louisa May Alcott

IWD!

CECILY

Guysssss

1st of all I decided I'm not using emojis anymore

I know it's awk but I am just over them

And I don't have the time bc I have so much hw

GABRIELLE

OMG I KNOW SO MUCH HW

CECILY

Anyway

I was gonna wait 2 tell u until Mr. A approved this but I am so excited that I can't wait

PRIANKA

??

NO CLUE WIGO 😬 😬 😬

Also

CECILY

Lol ok

I want to have an event on Friday for International Women's Day celebrating all women

GABRIELLE

Ohhhhh so that's what IWD stands for LOL

CECILY

Ya

After all the stupid broboom stuff it became clear we need an event more than ever that will celebrate women & show how awesome we are

I was so angry but then I got fired up & really wanted to do something meaningful

Make a difference ya know

My mom & sis agreed 2 bake for it

Bake sale and all $$ goes to the women's shelter in town

Maybe ur parents want 2 help, too

GABRIELLE

This is happening fri ????????

I had no idea 😲😲😲😲

I feel so overwhelmed & out of it all the time 🙁😩😕😢😲😲😵😵

30

GABRIELLE

Why can't I ever keep up 🐱🐱

CECILY

No no

It hasn't been announced yet

I just realized IWD is Sunday so I wrote to Mr. A

PRIANKA

Ohhhh

GABRIELLE

But Mr. A didn't write back yet?

CECILY

No

But fingers crossed

GABRIELLE

Yes

GABRIELLE

Should we recruit more bakers ????

CECILY

Not yet

VICTORIA

This is such a good idea !!!!!!

Omg I love it 🤍🖤🤍💟

Girl power 4 life
👊👊👊👊💁💁💁💁💁💁

CECILY

Love the enthusiasm, Vic

VICTORIA

U knowwww ittttttt 👍👍👍

Also since u cut emojis I need to make up for ittttttt

Haha

K I'll keep u guys in the loop

Dear Journal,

I feel so in between with everything. I think that's
what happens in March. I'm at this in-between
time of the year where not much is happening but
everything is happening all at once. I guess that's
how life always is maybe. I don't know. I confuse

33

myself. I feel in between friends, too, though. Miriam and I are so close now and I'm close to the Hannahs, too, but not as much. And of course obviously Cece, Pri & Vic. And I think I am making it work but sometimes it still feels awkward. Maybe life was simpler with one group? Who knows. And then I have my friends from camp, too. And I am so excited to go back this summer. I feel like Miriam kind of wants to come but won't say it. So we'll see what happens with that.

I am also sooooo stressed with schoolwork. I hate it. Why do I even have to be in school? It's just soooo hard for me. It seems easier for everyone else and I don't get it.

OK, gotta go to bed.

Love, Gabs

- -

OMG

VICTORIA

U guysssss

U r not going 2 believe what I heard

Apparently Hannah F's bat mitzvah invites are going out soon & they're a model of her bedroom

CECILY

What????

VICTORIA

Like 3D model

Each person gets one!!!

GABRIELLE

For real!

GABRIELLE

This is true 💁🏻💁🏻

Her dad is driving around in their convertible to hand them out to everyone in town

The rest are being mailed

She told us @ Miriam's sleepover last week

VICTORIA

OMG 😲😲😲

GABRIELLE

I am crying rn bc my bat mitzvah will be so lame compared 2 everyone's 😭😭😭

My parents don't have that much $$

CECILY

Gabs, stop

GABRIELLE

No 4 real

GABRIELLE

& it's the last one so everyone will be so
over them by then

I hate my December bday & being the
youngest

PRIANKA

Wait hold on 😬😬😬

Still catching up

Stop texting LOL 😂🤣😂

Ok caught up

Omg her bat mitz will be fanciest one yet
🛍️🎀👑👸

I mean she's only turning 13

What's gonna happen with her sweet
16 & HS graduation or her wedding or
whatevsssss

PRIANKA

This is nuts

CECILY

Ya

I agree

I mean it's a big moment but still

Gabs, is she inviting the whole grade

GABRIELLE

IDK

Prob no 😬😬😬

Annie Goldfarb is the only one who has done that

Not that there have been so many yet LOL

CECILY

True

VICTORIA

Omg I really want 2 be invited

CECILY

Same

PRIANKA

Guys don't freak out

It's ok

Gabrielle, Miriam

G M

GABRIELLE

Mir?

MIRIAM

Yeah?

GABRIELLE

Do u know if everyone is going 2 be invited to Hannah F's bat mitz?

MIRIAM

Ummmm

What do u mean everyone

GABRIELLE

Whole grade

Specifically Pri, Cece, Vic

MIRIAM

Ummm

I doubt whole grade

She has a huge family 👩🏻

And tons of friends from school and camp and Hebrew school and dance team 👧🏻👧🏻👧🏻👦🏻👦🏻

40

GABRIELLE

Oh hmm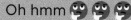

MIRIAM

IDK about Cece & Vic

She thinks Pri is hilarious btw so pos

GABRIELLE

Ok

MIRIAM

R u stressing ????

GABRIELLE

Kinda yeah

They're all talking about it

MIRIAM

Oh IDK

Sorry

Just ask her

41

GABRIELLE

I feel awk 😕 😕

MIRIAM

IKWYM

4 mine I def can't invite whole grade
😭 😭 🙀

GABRIELLE

Same 🙀 🙀 🙀

MIRIAM

At least we have a while 🙌 🙆‍♀️

GABRIELLE

Yeah def ✅ ✅ ✅

Hellllooooooo, Nickie & Kimmie!!!! ♡
(Remember when I used to call
you that?!)

Sending hugs from beautiful Yorkville.
I miss you guys!!! Are you doing an
International Women's Day celebration
at your school? My friend is trying to
start one here. So great, right? How
cute are the puppies on this postcard?
I found it at the grocery store.
LOVE YOU! Victoria

Nic a
c/o Land
AD
54 Clea
Philadelph

Mara, Cecily

MARA

I am sooooo excited about this IWD idea

Go you for thinking of it!!!

CECILY

Yeah so cool right?

Thank you!

MARA

I was thinking we could maybe bring in speakers, too

Like Yorkville mayor

She's friends with my mom

CECILY

Oh Mayor Baac

MARA

Yeah

They grew up together & still do yoga together once a week lol

CECILY

That's cool

I'm in

Just need approval from Mr. A

MARA

K please lmk

CECILY

Obv

From: Mr. Akiyama
To: Cecily Anderson
Subject: RE: International Women's Day

Dear Cecily,

What a fabulous idea! I discussed it with Mr. C and the administration and we all think it's great. Please stop by my office after school to discuss particulars. We only have a few days to get this going but we want to make it happen.

See you later,
Mr. A

***sent from my handheld device, please excuse any typos

IWD!

CECILY

Guys we r making this happen

I just met with Mr. A & he said yes

He loves bake sale fundraiser idea

PRIANKA

Wooooooo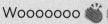

My mom will bake

VICTORIA

Actually my dad has this new cookie recipe

PRIANKA

Woo

VICTORIA

This is so awesome

GABRIELLE

What do we need to do ⁇

CECILY

Bring in posters + pictures of important women in ur life

& throughout history

& we're gonna hang them all over school

PRIANKA

Wow 👏👏👏🎉

CECILY

Mayor Baac is coming 2 speak

PRIANKA

That is so cool 🧜🧜👊👊👊

CECILY

& we r going to have an assembly with an open mic & people can come up 2 talk about women role models

PRIANKA

I am in love with this 🤍 🖤 🤍 💖

Go, CECE 📣 🤩 🎉 🎊

I'd say u'll be 1st women pres but I don't want to bc we better have a woman pres before u r old enough 🎉 🎉 🎉

VICTORIA

Um duh

CECILY

Thx, guys

I am so happy we could make this happen in only a few days

PRIANKA

CECE CAN RULE THE WORLD 🌍 🌍 🌍 🌎 🌎 🌎 🌎 🌎

CECILY

Lol ok stop

PRIANKA

4 real tho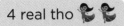

So proud of u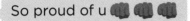

GABRIELLE

Same same same 👏👏👏

VICTORIA

U r amazing, Cece

CECILY

Guys sooooo much pressure when u say this stuff

Stopppp

Love u guys 🖤🖤🖤

Ack!! Used emojis by accident!

Sage, Prianka

SAGE

Omg why didn't we realize April was poetry month 🌸🌷🌹🥀🌺🌼🌻

PRIANKA

Ummm

I think I knew that

Maybe 🤪🤪

SAGE

Oh ok

PRIANKA

Do they do a thing @ school 4 it

SAGE

IDK

SAGE

Let's ask Ms. Marburn 2morrow since she's the head of the whole English dept

PRIANKA

Sounds good 💃💃

Ooooh end of the year poetry jam competition 👏👏👏

SAGE

U r so competitive 🙄

PRIANKA

Not really

SAGE

Ok

PRIANKA

But end of yr poetry jam could be so fun 🎉🎉🎉

SAGE

Yeah true 👍👍👍

SAGE

Like ☕☕ house setup

PRIANKA

LOL kids drinking coffee

SAGE

No soda & fruit punch but YKWIM 😬😬

PRIANKA

Yeah def hahaha 👏👏

Cece has totally inspired me to just start stuff 👊👊

Did I tell u she started this International Women's Day thing @ school

It's happening fri

SAGE

OMG NO but wowwwwww

PRIANKA

She just makes things happen ya know???

Let's do this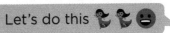

K see u tomorrow

Miriam, Gabrielle

Ok I spoke to Hannah 💭💭

She's not inviting whole grade

& of ur friends she's only inviting u & Pri

I mean u r Hannah's close friend now, too

YKWIM 😐

GABRIELLE

Yeah

What should I do

Should I tell my friends ahead of time

MIRIAM

No

Wait until invites go out

GABRIELLE

I feel so bad

MIRIAM

I do 2 but it's how it is

She really doesn't know Cece & Vic

She's not in any classes with them 📚📖

55

GABRIELLE

Well Cece is in all honors classes

MIRIAM

So she'll def be invited to Hannah P's then

GABRIELLE

Haha true

They're both brainiacs

MIRIAM

LOL

K gotta finish hw

GABRIELLE

Bye

Dear Cecily,
Would you like to give
some opening remarks at
IWD? Please stop by my
office so we can discuss.
Mr. A

IWD! Woo!

C   P   G   V

VICTORIA

Did u see all the pictures already up

I have study hall in the comp lab &
Mr. Surrey let us print pictures

VICTORIA

He never lets us do that

CECILY

Whoa that is so cool

I saw a lot already up

I hope more people hang stuff

Mr. A said we can leave them up all next week

VICTORIA

I love this

CECILY

& Mr. A said I can give opening remarks

PRIANKA

Wowwwieeeeeeeeee

CECILY

Ya

CECILY

Gtg work on that

Bye

PRIANKA

Mwaaaahhhhhhhhhhhh

Gabrielle, Cecily

GABRIELLE

Cece?

CECILY

Ya

GABRIELLE

Just wanted to thank u for coming over

GABRIELLE

I know you're so busy with IWD & it was late but you helped me sooooooo much with that math hw 👏👏👏

TBH you teach better than our actual teachers LOL 😛😛

CECILY

IDK about that but you're welcome!!

GABRIELLE

Love you, Cece 🖤🖤🖤

CECILY

Mwah!!!!!!

Draft—Opening remarks for International
Women's Day
Cecily Anderson

Hi, everyone! Welcome, students, faculty, and community members, to Yorkville Middle School's first-ever International Women's Day celebration. I am so excited that we are all here.

My name is Cecily Anderson. International Women's Day sort of snuck up on me this year, so we had to throw this celebration together on short notice. I'm so grateful to Mr. Akiyama and Mr. Carransey for helping pull this off.

Our hallways are covered with photos of inspiring women and it looks incredible. We are also so fortunate to have Yorkville's amazing mayor, Esme Baac, with us.

I'll keep my remarks short so we can start the program. I just wanted to say that women are out there in this world every single day doing important, meaningful things and very often they go unnoticed. We need to make sure we're celebrating women and encouraging girls to be all they can be and change the world. We can do this.

I kept hearing things in the hallway that really got me angry and fired up. In a way, I'm glad, though, because it inspired this celebration of women!

After Mayor Baac speaks, we'll have an open mic opportunity for students to come up and speak about women heroes and role models. Please keep it brief but passionate.

Thanks everyone! Happy International Women's Day!

HIIIIIIII

ELOISE

Guess what

MIRIAM

??

ELOISE

U know how my aunt is a producer @ the today show

HANNAH F

Haha yessssss

U have told us a billion times LOL

ELOISE

K stop

ELOISE

Anyway i told her about international women's day celebration @ school

ELOISE

And how it all came together super quickly

And how all the admin people were into the idea

& she's coming to produce a spot on it for the show! 🧛🧛😀😀

MIRIAM

OMG 😵😵😵😱

R we all gonna be on TV 📺📺

ELOISE

Maybeee!!!!!!! 🧛🧛😀😀👊👊

GABRIELLE

Did u tell Cece

She started this whole thing and it was all her idea and she is so so into it

ELOISE

Oh really

ELOISE

I didn't know that

Can u tell her

I don't really know her

GABRIELLE

Let's tell her in person tomorrow morning

Too confusing 2 text

ELOISE

K

HANNAH P

That is so so so so cool, El!

ELOISE

I'm so excited

HANNAH P

U should be

I can tell Cecily, too

HANNAH P

We have all classes together this year

MIRIAM

Love all of this 🤍🖤🤍🖤

GABRIELLE

Me too 💃💃👍👍👍

Dear Journal,

It's 3 a.m. and I can't fall asleep. I really need to, though. Tomorrow is our big International Women's Day event and it was all my idea and I'm making opening remarks and I want to be well rested. But I can't sleep! Wahhhhh!!! I am just so excited that they listened to me and took my idea and it's really happening. I don't know what else to say really.

I also really want to be invited to Hannah F's bat mitzvah. It's going to be so amazing. I heard she's giving out hoodies. Like real nice ones with our names on them. I don't understand how her parents have so much money. Mine are just regular people and we're fine but not rich. Sometimes it seems like everyone else is so rich. And the people at school who aren't just don't say anything. It's like we all just pretend everyone's family can afford to do all this big stuff. We should discuss it more. I am so nervous I won't be invited and everyone else will. I am trying to stay calm about it but I really want to go. I keep picturing how fancy it will be.

Okay, I am going to try and go to bed again.

Love, Cecily

Dearest Cecily,

I am so proud of you and all you have accomplished with International Women's Day. I want you to know that I adore you just the way you are and think you're extraordinary. You follow your passions and you work hard and you're kind. I am so grateful that I get to be your mother.

I love you, Mom

Mara, Cecily

MARA

OMG

Do u know about our moms

CECILY

What?

Walking out the door 2 the bus rn

R u already there

MARA

Yeah early as usual LOL

CECILY

K I can walk & text

MARA

Be careful

K but what about our moms

MARA

Ummm this is so awk & embarrassing

CECILY

Tell me rn

I am nervous

MARA

They knew about us

CECILY

WDYM

MARA

Like how we kinda liked each other but how we are just friends now

CECILY

OMG

They did

How???

No idea

Mom intuition I guess

Did u tell ur mom

Nooooooo

I'd never discuss personal stuff w/ her

I didn't, either

My mom did leave me a super gushy note today

??

Like how she's so proud of me & how I should always stay true to myself

Omg

I KNOW

Ewwww I don't like moms knowing about love stuff

This is love stuff?????

YKWIM

I know . . . crushes etc

Right

MARA

But we r just friends now

CECILY

Duh I know

MARA

Ok ha

CECILY

Hahahahahahahahah

MARA

I see u walking here

CECILY

LOL k bye

Cece, I lost my voice & I can't talk at all.
I don't know what happened! I feel fine,
though. Anyway, Eloise's aunt works for
the Today show & they're coming to do
a piece on IWD!!! She told me last night.
She's going to tell u in person today but I
wanted to tell u first. OMG RIGHT?
Xoxoxoxoxxoxo love, Gabs

For real? This is so amazing. She cleared it with Mr. A & Mr. C and everyone?

I think so!

Wowwwwwwwwwwwww I am sooooooo excited but also sooooo nervous now, too.

Me too! What if we become famous?

We'll be amazing! We already are!

AHHHHHH!!!!!!

Dear Students & Parents:

A film crew from the *Today* show will be at Yorkville Middle School recording the International Women's Day events tomorrow. Please e-sign below and then email back the form if you would like to allow your child to appear on television.

Thank you,
Yorkville Middle School Administration

I, _____, allow my child, _____, to appear on the *Today* show in connection with Yorkville Middle School's International Women's Day event.

Signed,

_____
(Parent/guardian signature)

Hi, guys—Do you guys realize how few pages we have left in shared notebook?!? Like, fewer than 10. OMG. So...hiiiii!!!! So proud of Cece & just want u guys to know I love you! I may read a poem @ the open mic part. Maybe. Xoxo Pri

Oooh, that's such a good idea, Pri! I don't know if I'll do anything. Luv, VM

I can't do anything because I lost my voice! Today of all days. How crazy? Wahhhh!!! Smooches, Gabs

Don't worry, it'll all be great!!!! LOVE YOU ALL!!!!!!!! Xoxoxoxo Cece

Prianka Basak's IWD Poem:

Think hard about who has played a major role
   in your life.
It's a woman, right?
Your mom, of course
Your grandma
An aunt
A teacher
A friend
It doesn't matter their exact title
It matters what they do
How they live
Their actions
Their words
A comforting hug
A smile when you need it most
Someone to say "you can do this"
   "you've got this"

Someone who can tell you're hurting
    before you've even said a word
These are the ladies changing the world
Not by being famous
Just by being themselves
By spreading kindness
Each little drop of kindness
    goes so far
So say thank you
    today
And every day
To all the women heroes
    in your life

Hi, everyone. My name is Mae Revis and I don't usually speak at these things but here goes. I want to talk about my grandma Sylvia Taracci. She has picked me up every day after school since preschool. And even now when I am old enough to walk home alone, she waits for me at home with my favorite passion fruit tea and cookies. Every day. Without my grandma Sylvia, my mom wouldn't be able to work. My mom loves her job as an occupational therapist but sometimes the hours can vary because she sees patients in their homes. My grandma Sylvia is my hero because she helps my mom and helps me at the same time. I thank her on Mother's Day and on her birthday but I should really thank her every day for her selflessness and generosity.

Eloise, Cecily

MAYBE: ELOISE

Cecily! Today was so great!

My aunt was realllllllly impressed

CECILY

OMG thanks so much!

MAYBE: ELOISE

For real u did so great

CECILY

Thank you!

MAYBE: ELOISE

I know we don't really know each other and all that stuff happened with Sami but Gabs is so awesome and she loves u and after today I feel like u r awesome, too

CECILY

Hahahahahaha thanks

I really appreciate that, Eloise!

I'm adding you to my phone

ELOISE

U r welcome 💃💃

Great job 🤸🤸🤸🤸

CECILY

Thx

Vishal, Prianka

VISHAL

Today was cool

PRIANKA

I agree

VISHAL

I get what u r saying about women's history month now

PRIANKA

You do?

VISHAL

Yeah

PRIANKA

Good

Better late than never

VISHAL

Ya

PRIANKA

Appreciate u telling me that

I gotta run now tho

VISHAL

Peace

Gabrielle, Cecily

GABRIELLE

Hey did Eloise text u ❓

She asked me for ur number 📱

CECILY

Yeah she did

So nice

GABRIELLE

U really crushed it today, Cece

Everyone got so into it

U could hear a pin drop in the auditorium
👀 😐 🤐

CECILY

Hahaha I know

Even the boys were into it

Which is amazing bc I alluded to the broboom stuff

I was scared to do it but it felt right

GABRIELLE

So proud of you for doing that

85

Did u hear what Jared Remington had to say about his aunt who overcame cancer as a kid and went on to be an Olympic swimmer

GABRIELLE

I know

So incredible 👊 👊

Was such a great day 💯 💯 💯

Are u happy with it all

CECILY

Kinda but not totally

Can I be honest

GABRIELLE

Um sure

CECILY

Ok well

86

I didn't want to tell Eloise this but

I never got to be interviewed for the today show

I was running around making sure the bake sale was all set and the speakers and Mayor Baac & then the TV crew had to leave

GABRIELLE

Oh no, Cece

CECILY

I didn't want to complain to Eloise but I am so sad

I feel like I worked so hard & I really wanted to do that part

GABRIELLE

Yeah that stinks

I don't even know what to say

GABRIELLE

The whole thing was your idea

I bet they tried to find you

CECILY

Yeah IDK

GABRIELLE

Love u, Cece 🖤🖤🖤

U r amazing and u made this whole thing happen and u help everyone all the time

CECILY

Thank you

Love u too

Prianka, Cecily

PRIANKA

Hey, Cece 👋🏽👋🏾👋🏼

CECILY

Hey

PRIANKA

The IWD event was so great 🎉🎉🎉

CECILY

Thank you

PRIANKA

I wondered if u wanted to help me get the poetry month thing going

Sage & I have ideas but we need your help to make things happen LOL 😬😬😬😂🤣

Haha ok

Sure I guess

K talk tomorrow

Love you!!! 🖤 🖤

From: Summer in Maine Volunteer Corps Staff
To: Summer in Maine Volunteer Corps Attendees
Subject: Summer 2020

Hello!

We are so excited to officially welcome you to Summer in Maine Volunteer Corps! You'll be receiving much more information at the end of April about what to pack and how to prepare for the summer. Until then, we want to get a sense of your preferences about volunteering specifics. We'll have various projects going on at the same time.

1. Volunteer with the residents at the local nursing home. Each Volunteer Corps attendee will be paired with a resident.

2. Help repair neighborhood homes damaged from recent storms.

3. Help with the exterior and interior painting of the local community center.

We may have a few more projects lined up. Stay tuned for more information.

Best wishes,
Summer Volunteer Corps Staff

VC CREW!

M C M

MAE

Hiiiii

Which project r u guys gonna do ⁉️

CECILY

Hiii

I didn't know u were def coming to volunteer corps with us

MAE

Oh haha

Yeah I am

MARA

I told u that, Cece

CECILY

I thought it was a maybe

MARA

Oh

Do u not want me to come?

CECILY

Nooooo of course I do

MARA

I think I'm gonna do painting

I heard we'll be able to do murals and stuff

MAE

Oh cool 🖌️ 🎨 🎨 🖼️

I wanna do that 2 🎨 🎨

CECILY

I think I'll do nursing home

MAE

I hope we can all do the same thing

MARA

Is Victoria coming?

CECILY

Maybe but IDK for sure yet

What is Marissa doing this summer?

U guys will be apart!!!

MARA

Ha we were apart last yr when I was @ camp duh

CECILY

Right

MAE

Marissa is going to stay with her grandparents near Washington DC all summer 🌍 🌎

Her mom is on some assignment there 📒 📒

CECILY

Oh

MAE

K lmk what u guys sign up for 👊 👊

Cece, u can guide us

CECILY

Lol why

MAE

IDK u just have stuff figured out

CECILY

IDK about that

MARA

I gtg

CECILY

Bye

MAE

Xoxox

WHOAAAA

PRIANKA

U guys this invite is even crazier than I expected 😵😵😵

CECILY

??

VICTORIA

What invite ??!!!

Prianka, Gabrielle

PRIANKA

Gabs ???

GABRIELLE

Yeah ????

PRIANKA

Did u get the invite for Hannah F's bat mitz

GABRIELLE

Yeah

PRIANKA

I don't think Cece & Vic did

GABRIELLE

Ummm

PRIANKA

What

97

GABRIELLE

Yeah when I asked Mir she said she didn't think they'd be invited 😨😨😨

HF doesn't really know them 🤪🤪🤪

PRIANKA

I don't know her that well

GABRIELLE

But u have classes together

She thinks u r really funny 😂🤣😂

PRIANKA

She does? 🙈🙂🙃🙂

GABRIELLE

Haha yeah

PRIANKA

Flattered but what do we do about Cece and Vic

GABRIELLE

IDK

98

I didn't answer just now

I know

Hmmm

I have been stressing about this

Does this one seem like a bigger deal than the others

We weren't invited to Ayelet Birnbaum's and we didn't care that much

& Cece was invited to hers

IK

This one feels diff tho bc everyone is talking about it

PRIANKA

Yeah true

Why is this one so fancy

GABRIELLE

IDK

Her grandparents are really rich & they pay for everything 🤑🤑

PRIANKA

Omg how do u know this

I never know stuff like this

GABRIELLE

IDK

Mir & her friends talk about weird stuff like money 👧👧

IDK

PRIANKA

I love how u call her Mir

Like u r just sooooo close LOL

GABRIELLE

Ew stop

We r close, Pri!! 👧👧👧👧

PRIANKA

I know jk 😝 😝

I'm just saying

It's funny

GABRIELLE

Fine whatever

PRIANKA

Don't be so sensitive, Gabs

GABRIELLE

I'm not

PRIANKA

Fine whatever LOL

GABRIELLE

STOP

We have a big issue here

PRIANKA

Yeah

But remember when I wasn't invited to the party at the Mexican restaurant in 5th grade

Those twins who moved away

GABRIELLE

Yeah Cassidy and Genevieve

PRIANKA

Right good memory

So it was a bummer I wasn't invited

But my mom was like

PRIANKA

Listen, Prianka darling, not everyone gets invited to every social gathering

That is a fact of life

It is painful

But we move forward

GABRIELLE

Ha

U remember that word for word

PRIANKA

Kinda yeah

It stayed with me

I think she was right

GABRIELLE

Mama Basak is always right

Def true

She is a wise 🇮🇳 🇮🇳 goddess

Hahaha 😂 😂

We have to answer them

IK

So answer them

No u

Waahhhh

Wahhhhhhhhh 😿 😿 😿 😿

WHOAAAA

PRIANKA

The HF bat mitz invite

CECILY

I didn't get it

VICTORIA

Neither did I

GABRIELLE

I don't think everyone was invited so don't feel bad 🤍🖤🤍💖

Cece & Vic, u don't really know her

PRIANKA

Yeah don't feel bad at all

VICTORIA

Easy for u to say 😿😿😿🐱🐱

U guys were invited 🐱🐱

PRIANKA

Not everyone gets invited to everything in life 🐱🐱

Just how it goes 🙅🏻‍♀️🙅🏻‍♀️🙆‍♀️🙅🏻‍♀️🙅🏻‍♀️🙆‍♀️

VICTORIA

Still hurts tho 😨😦

CECILY

It does hurt

Especially bc this one sounds so fab

VICTORIA

Yeah ☝🏼

PRIANKA

Cece, u rarely care about this stuff

CECILY

I know

I do care tho

I can admit when I care

I missed out on the today show thing & now this

GABRIELLE

That's healthy 💁‍♀️💁‍♀️

To say how you're feeling I mean

Sorry this is happening 😬😬😬

VICTORIA

I am bummed 😦😦

PRIANKA

Vic, don't tell ur mom and make everything crazy 😛😛😂🤣😂

VICTORIA

OMG that is rude, Pri 😟😦😫😣😖😫 😵😈😈

I wouldn't 😫😩😫😩

107

PRIANKA

Sorry didn't mean to be rude

Ur mom has a good

But she gets so upset when u r hurt

VICTORIA

That's true

GABRIELLE

It's true that not everyone can be invited all
the time tho

Literal fact of life

CECILY

We get that, Gabs

I gtg

VICTORIA

Same

GABRIELLE

LOVE U ALL

PRIANKA

Mwahhhhhhhh

Victoria, Cecily

VICTORIA

They think they r so cool bc they got
invited 😬😬😬😖😫😭😿

CECILY

Vicccccccc

Don't go there

VICTORIA

What 😫 😫

It's true

CECILY

Gabs is very close with HF

And Pri is in classes with her

We're not

VICTORIA

Technically I have gym with her

But she always gets out of playing

CECILY

Seriously??

VICTORIA

Yeah she always has a note

IDK why

CECILY

Oh weird

110

VICTORIA

I want to go thoooooo

CECILY

Same but what can we do

We can hang out ourselves that night

Go to a movie or something

Maybe bowling

VICTORIA

I know but still

CECILY

We gotta stay chill about it

If we let on we're upset it makes it worse

VICTORIA

It does?

CECILY

Ya

CECILY

Focus on other stuff

R u doing summer volunteer corps

VICTORIA

My parents are still discussing

I think so tho

CECILY

Cool

U could prob go for just 1 session & still have time for Philly & stuff

VICTORIA

Yeah maybe

At least I have u

I feel like u always know what to say in all situations

CECILY

So not true but ok

CECILY

I am pretty bummed tbh

VICTORIA

U r a rock tho

4 real

CECILY

Whatever u say

Prianka, Gabrielle

PRIANKA

Soooooo

I feel so bad about this but 😬😬😬

I am also so so so excited for Hannah's bat mitz

GABRIELLE

OMG same 🙌🙏🙌

But I do feel bad 🙄🙄🙄😿

Is Sage invited

PRIANKA

Yeah but that's bc they r in Hebrew school together

GABRIELLE

Oh yeah

GABRIELLE

Is Sage having a really fancy one

PRIANKA

IDK

I feel bad tho bc no side chats duh

& here we r side chatting

But it would be mean to rub their faces in it ya know

GABRIELLE

Totally

We shouldn't mention it at all

PRIANKA

Agree ✅✅✅

GABRIELLE

This is def an apart but still together deal

PRIANKA

OMG I love that

PRIANKA

That may be our tagline

GABRIELLE

LOL what

PRIANKA

Like tagline 4 our group

GABRIELLE

Ok sounds good 😊 😊

PRIANKA

Gonna write a poem

Brb

GABRIELLE

K

Hi, Cece—

Check out this article I found. Moms and daughters keep these journals together and they discuss all the hard things that can sometimes be difficult to talk about in person. I know you already have a journal that you got as a present but maybe you would want to do this, too? Give it a read and let me know what you think.

I love you, Mom

Prianka, Sage

P   S

PRIANKA

OMG best idea ever just came to me 💡💡💡💡💡

SAGE

Describe!

PRIANKA

For poetry month

We have bowls of mini poems around the school

& students pick up a poem and read it and then pass it to someone

SAGE

Sounds so cool 👍👍👍

We need to have our meeting to discuss all the stuff we want to do

PRIANKA

I know

Let's fig out a time tomorrow

I can see when Cece is free to help us

SAGE

K sounds good

PRIANKA

Mwah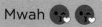

SAGE

Mwah

Prianka, Cecily

PRIANKA

Hey

CECILY

Hiiiii

PRIANKA

Can u meet w/ Sage & me to discuss
poetry month and help us

CECILY

Pri, u totally got this

U can do it & I don't think u need my help

PRIANKA

Ummmmm

CECILY

For real

CECILY

I have faith in you

PRIANKA

Ok

CECILY

Not doing it to be mean, just have a lot
going on and I truly think you'll be great

PRIANKA

K love you

CECILY

Love you, too

~~~~~~

Dear Journal,

We have to do an entry during English today and even
though this is really something I'd write in my journal
at home I'll write it here since Mr. Cental says he

doesn't read our journal entries. I believe him. He's very honest. You can tell by his eyes. Anyway, onto my entry. I am so upset about this Hannah bat mitzvah thing but I am trying to play it cool. I don't want Victoria to get all worked up and then go crying to her mom and cause some crazy drama. Pri's right that it's a fact of life that not every person is invited to every event. It's just how it is. But even when something is a fact of life it still feels really painful. I want to go to that party, too, and get dressed up and enjoy all the fancy stuff. It just sounds like so much fun. Ugh, I am getting upset now just writing this. I feel like I could cry and I really don't want to cry in class. I guess I'll just cut this off. I'm so proud of all I accomplished with IWD and bringing up the broboom thing but then I'm so sad about this bat mitzvah drama. It feels uneven. I really really hope you're not reading this, Mr. Cental.

Bye. XOXOXO
Cece

Omg, Pri, what if each day of poetry month we had a different poetry-related thing?

YESSSS! Love that, Sage. In love with it. OMG YES YESSSSSSS

Can we think of thirty poetry-related activities, though?

YES, of course we can. First of all, the pick a poem thing, from the bowls. Then we can also have a poetry wall one day where people just scribble up short poems. Maybe a dry erase? Or a chalkboard? One day we'll have people bring in their favorite poem and hang it up. One day we'll have an open mic poetry slam thing. Um, how many is that? Okay, so we'll need more. Maybe a day where we focus on all the national poet laureate (did I spell that right?) people? And then also a day for books in verse? Songs that are poems one day? SO MANY IDEAS. I am on fiiireeeeee, baby. I am so inspired by what Cece did with IWD and making it happen & I want to start things & make things happen, too! POETRY PALS for LIFE!!!!!!!!!!!!!!!!

Okay, got it. I love you, Pri. You're so awesome.

Duh. I know I am. Okay, you are, too.

LOL K.

:) :) :)

VC Crew!!!!

MAE
Hiiii

VICTORIA
Hiii

MAE
So excited for summer volunteer corps

VICTORIA
Me tooo

MAE

Did we all agree to do the same project

MARA

I am still deciding

CECILY

Hi same

MAE

Ok

Am kinda scared bc I only know u guys

And we are going far away

Kids from all over the country

VICTORIA

It'll be totes fine

CECILY

Def

MAE

K but I kinda want to stay together if pos 👧👧👧👧

VICTORIA

K we'll do best we can ❗❗❗

MARA

Mae u gotta chill

It's gonna be fine, dude

MAE

Dude ❓❓❓❓❓❓❓❓❓❓

Who r u rn ❓❓

MARA

LOL IDK

But u r acting looney tuneeeesssss

MAE

I'm fine 👊 👊

K bye 👋 👋 👋

Cecily, Ingrid

CECILY

Ing?

R u home

I could get up from my bed and see but I am too lazy

INGRID

Almost home

Went for a run

CECILY

U r running & texting @ the same time

INGRID

NO LOL

Cool-down walk

INGRID

You ok?

CECILY

Yes come by my room when u get home

Wanna talk 2 u

INGRID

Sure you're ok?

CECILY

Yes

3:31 PM

INGRID

Wait why are you texting me when we are standing right next to each other

CECILY

Bc Mom is def eavesdropping

But she'll prob see these texts

She has that app where she can see all my texts

129

That's why I delete them all right away

Not that I have so many secrets but YKWIM

We can't hide from our all-knowing, snooping mama...

INGRID

K hold

So what's going on?

OK, writing is slower than texting but prob safer. Be patient. So all of this stuff feels like no big deal but then when I add it all up it really starts to upset me and stress me out. I think Mom is on this weird concerned-about-me stretch so I am trying to not make her more concerned which is why I didn't want to talk out loud.

Okay... So talk to me. Or I mean write to me. Ha!

Well, first of all, it was just supposed to be Mara and me going to the volunteer summer corps thing but now Victoria is coming, too, and so is Mae, and it feels like too many people going to something together. I like to branch out and meet new people and Mae is already stressing that she doesn't know anyone and can we do everything together and blah blah blah.

Okay. Got that. Tell me everything at once and then I can address each issue.

Okay. So there's that. And also I wasn't invited to Hannah Fletch's bat mitzvah and I really wanted to be. It's gonna be super fancy and fun and I am so so upset I wasn't invited. Pri and Gabs were but Victoria wasn't and I'm trying to stay chill but still so upset. So that's another thing. Also I just feel like everyone is always leaning on me and saying how I know everything and can rule the world but it's too much. I guess those are the main issues but I wanted to talk to you about them.

Okay. Well, first of all, I get the thing with Mae and the trip. But this is always what happens. There's tons of anxiety before you go and when you get there it's totally fine. She'll probably branch out a little and you obviously will and everyone will get settled and it will be fine. I don't think she'll hang on you for the entire time.

As for the bat mitzvah, yeah, it sucks. That definitely happened to me a bunch and it was really upsetting. I remember when everyone in the grade got invited to Becca Emanuel's. Well, I guess not everyone, but it felt like that and I was so bummed. I made Mom and Dad sit up with me until like 1 a.m. one night crying about it. Seriously! Do you remember this? It was a big deal at the time but then everyone got over it, including me. Maybe the kids at school wore the giveaway for one day and that was it. I mean, it's not fun to not be included, but you're right, it is something that will happen. Here's the thing, Cece my love. You're awesome. You did such a fab job with the International Women's Day thing. And you're def the smartest kid in the grade and you're just amazing. Middle school isn't the best and you're still crushing it. Middle school is just this weird in-between little slice of life that's awkward and messy and frankly kind of dumb. Everyone just wants to get through it, but you're really making a difference! You're doing more than just getting through it. And that's why people look to you so much. You're such a role model! Of course that's hard.

And yeah, it sucks about Hannah Fletch, but it's not like you were ever really friends with her. And isn't it kind of weird to have that fancy of a party for a thirteen-year-old? I mean, it is weird. And the whole thing that went down with her friend Sami— best to stay away from that group, if you want my honest opinion. So what else can I tell you?

Yeah, I do kind of remember. Ingrid, my wise and amazing older sister, what would I ever do without you?

I'm so glad we had this "chat." I really should come and talk to you more often, LOL. Can we do a sister sleepover like we used to when we were little and camp out in one of our rooms in sleeping bags on the floor and try to stay up late?

Sure, that would be fabulous. Name the time and I'm there.

K, will do.

Also I still need to watch the clip from the IWD thing on the Today show. I know they didn't interview you and you're still upset but YOU MADE THE WHOLE THING HAPPEN. And I am so proud. Viewing party tonight?

YES FAB YES

Ingrid, Cecily

INGRID

K, my hand is tired from writing. Going to get a snack. Also do I smell from my run? How have you been this close to me this whole time?

CECILY

You don't smell. I promise.

INGRID

K, but I still need to shower

CECILY

Yes, good plan. Love you!

INGRID

Love you!

MISS & LOVE U GUYS

VICTORIA

Guys?

I feel like we've barely texted recently

Where is everyone‼️!

PRIANKA

Hi

Very busy with poetry   planning

Gonna be soooo sooo awesome

Cece, u and IWD were my inspiration

I wanted to plan something, too, LOL

VICTORIA

Woo 🎉🎉🎉🎉🎉

GABRIELLE

I'm here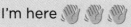

Feeling overwhelmed with hw tho

Why is this half of the year so much more work 😿😭😿🐱🧑

And all of it is sooooo hard 😫😐😫😐

VICTORIA

CECILY

I'm here

Have been feeling a little blah

PRIANKA

For real, Cece?

CECILY

Ya

PRIANKA

Whyyyyyyyy 🙀🙀🙀🙀

CECILY

IDK really

GABRIELLE

Cece, we are here for u 👭👭👭

CECILY

Thanks

VICTORIA

Oh no, Cece, my summer buddy

CECILY

Ha

VICTORIA

U r my summer buddy right? 🙌🙏🙌🙇

CECILY

Haha ya

PRIANKA

Back to poetry planning

Talk later, peeps

GABRIELLE

Mwahhhhhhh

VICTORIA

Lates, peeeeps

Can I make lates a thing

GABRIELLE

Lol IDK

PRIANKA

Bye 4 real now

Hi, friends!!!!

Hello, it's meeeee!!!! YOUR BFF SINCE PRESCHOOL, VICTORIA MELFORD, and POSTCARD PAL!!!! I miss you soooooo much. I think I am doing this super awesome volunteer corps thing this summer with one of my new besties here, Cecily. You met her! Remember? So yeah. I'm not sure if I'll be in Philly at all. Maybe for a weekend when we come to visit my grandma, but I think that's it. How's everything there? Fill me in. I really miss you guys.

LOVE YOU FOREVS!

Victoria Melford

Nic a

c/o

54 C

Phila

OUTDOOR EXPLORERS

HELLO!

Outdoor Explorers REUNION IS SO SOON!! We're planning a fun get-together! Please save the date! Saturday, April 25, at 11 a.m. in Central Park by the boathouse! Bring a picnic lunch and some fun stories to share. See you soon!

Love and hugs,
Your Outdoor Explorers Summer 2020 counselors

Darren, Aviva, George, Marley, Everett, and Vee

Ivy, Gabrielle

IVY

OMGGGG 😯 😯 😯

I am soooooo excited for this 🎉 🎉 🎉

And in NYC aka my fave place in the world 🍎 🗽 🏙️

GABRIELLE

I know! U love NYC!

IVY

Yeahhhhhhh

GABRIELLE

So fun 😀 😀 😀 😀

I am so excited

IVY

Is this only for this summer people or last summer, too

GABRIELLE

I think only this summer

IVY

Eli is coming back btw

GABRIELLE

Oh cool

IVY

I am sooooooo excited

GABRIELLE

Me too

Summer feels like so far away, though

IVY

Yeah IKWYM

GABRIELLE

I am having so much trouble in school

I am kinda hiding it

I haven't told my friends or my mom or dad 😭😭😭

I just keep thinking I will get through it

IVY

Oh noooo, Gabs

What can I do to help

GABRIELLE

IDK

I should prob talk to my mom

But I hate to worry her

IVY

But she's ur mom and that's her job

GABRIELLE

I know but still

GABRIELLE

My teachers are prob gonna call her soon

I just can't keep up with the work

And my friends are so smart

So I feel so dumb 😭 😢 😢 🙀 🙀

IVY

Gabs, don't say that

You're awesome

And people can help you

GABRIELLE

Ughhhhh

I just don't understand how it got so hard so fast 😬 😬 😬

Like out of nowhere

IVY

Maybe it's just a lot all at once?

GABRIELLE

Maybe

But I can't even understand what we are doing in math

And I feel like there are so many tests

And we have been doing short stories in English and even they're confusing

And this poetry unit is gonna be impossibleeeeeee

IVY

Sounds super stressful

Sorry you're going thru this

GABRIELLE

Thx

I better study

Ily

IVY

Ily2

Prianka, Gabrielle

PRIANKA

Gabs

R u still up

GABRIELLE

Yeah ughhh

So much hw

Really? I feel like it wasn't that much

Oh IDK

What's up ❓❓❓❓

Do u want to go dress shopping together for Hannah F's bat mitz 👗👗👗👗

Since it's our first black tie one my mom said I could get a new dress

Maybe ur mom wants to come, too

Oh maybe

This sounds awesome 🧜🧜🧜🧜

I'll have Mama Basak talk to ur mom

GABRIELLE

K

Sounds great

Back to hw

Xoxo 🖤🖤🖤

PRIANKA

Nighty night 😴😴😴

From: Gabrielle Katz
To: Evelyn Brickfeld
Subject: Meeting

Hi, Ms. Brickfeld,

I wondered if I could meet with you during lunch today or tomorrow. Please let me know.

Thanks, Gabby

Hi, Pri–

Tell everyone I'm meeting Ms. Brickfeld in guidance at lunch. Remember no chatting about HF's bat mitz. K? I feel like Cece's feelings are hurt. Love you, Gabs

Gabrielle, Ivy

G I

GABRIELLE

Ivy, r u there ?

Ik it's the middle of school day

But sometimes I sneak and check my phone

K guess u r not

Talk later

Need to talk to u

From: Cecily Anderson
To: Summer in Maine Volunteer Corps Staff
Subject: Question

Hello,

My name is Cecily Anderson and I signed up to be part of the Summer in Maine Volunteer Corps. I was so lucky to get a scholarship and I am so grateful. However, some scheduling glitches have come up and I may not be able to attend. I wondered also about your cancellation policy. I hope another student can get the scholarship and enjoy the opportunity. Please get back to me.

Thank you,
Cecily Anderson

I'm not afraid of storms, for I'm learning how to sail my ship.
—Louisa May Alcott

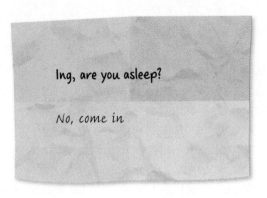

Ing, are you asleep?

No, come in

From: Ingrid Anderson
To: Cecily Anderson
Subject: thoughts

Cece,

I'm emailing you because I'm in study hall and I finished all my work and I have been thinking about our talk last night. I'll be home late because I have drama club and I wanted to make sure I got back to you.

I totally see what you're saying. I also see the dilemma. I get that you feel stuck and I get that you feel obligated to follow through with these plans. But in all fairness, you made them on your own and then others joined in. Sometimes I do think you need to go with your gut feeling. If you think you're not going to enjoy the program, you should skip it. There are other options for the summer.

I know you always feel a loyalty to friends and that's what makes you so amazing, but sometimes you do have to look out for yourself, too. Also can I just say how happy I am that you're coming to me with all of these things? I really feel like we've gotten closer in the past year and I am so, so happy about that. I'm so proud of you, Cece, and I love you so much.

X Ingrid

Gabs, hope all is okay with guidance and everything. I'm so, so sorry but I think I did talk about HF and the bat mitzvah too much. Victoria kept asking me questions! It's like she wants to torture herself about it. And then Sage came over to our table talking about it and it all kind of unraveled. I'm really sorry. Text me later to discuss in more detail. Xox Pri

Gabrielle, Prianka

G   P

GABRIELLE

Hey

Major drama going on that I haven't told anyone

PRIANKA

What ??

GABRIELLE

I feel like I may need to do summer school

I mean I don't have to

But Ms. Brickfeld says it could help

PRIANKA

OMG, Gabs

GABRIELLE

IK

Anyway what happened at lunch

PRIANKA

Everything went crazy

Vic is obsessed

She wouldn't stop asking me questions

PRIANKA

Miriam sat with us btw

So maybe that was why, too

IDK

GABRIELLE

So what happened

PRIANKA

Well Cece started crying

I mean in her Cece way where you can't really tell but I could tell

GABRIELLE

Yeah IKWYM

PRIANKA

So she left

And then Vic ran after her and it was all so awk and dumb

GABRIELLE

Ughhhhhhhh blarghshshshh

PRIANKA

Exactly

GABRIELLE

It'll be ok

I gtg

Wish I could talk more but drowning in hw

Feeling miserable

Love youuuuuu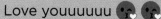

PRIANKA

Mwaaahhh

From: Summer in Maine Volunteer Corps Staff
To: Cecily Anderson
Subject: RE: Question

Dear Cecily,

We understand that things come up. We are grateful you reached out because we have a waiting list of scholarship applicants. Please let us know by Friday if you are definitely changing your mind about attending the program.

Best wishes,
Una Tolaf
Summer in Maine Volunteer Corps codirector

One must maintain a little bit of summer, even in the middle of winter.
—Henry David Thoreau

SPINE POETRY CONTEST!

Grab some books from the library
and make a poem out of their titles—
book spines facing you!

Get creative! Have fun!

Display your spine poetry on the shelf
in the library!

First, second, and third place
will receive prizes.

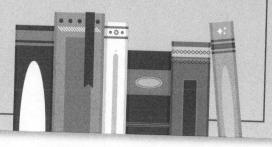

Prianka, Cecily

PRIANKA

Cece 👋🏾👋🏾👋🏾

U around ❓❓

Just wanted to check in

CECILY

Hi

PRIANKA

How are u

CECILY

Ehh

I've been better

PRIANKA

Ugh, Cece, I'm sorry 🙄😫😣🙀

CECILY

Not ur fault obvs

PRIANKA

Ik but still

CECILY

It's a lot of stuff

Not just the Hannah F bat mitz

PRIANKA

What else

CECILY

IDK

I just feel like everyone leans on me

All the time

PRIANKA

I'm sorry

I leaned on u with poetry stuff

That's not the main issue

I just need space

Do u want to talk

Not rn

But thanks

K

Love u, Cece 🖤🖤🖤

Love u too

Dear Journal,

I am in the worst mood EVER. I don't usually get
like this, but when I do it's serious. And this is mega
serious! I am so annoyed at everyone. Well, I mean, not
everyone. Ingrid has been really helpful lately so that's
been good. But I am so annoyed at Victoria and I feel
like I can never say anything since she's so sensitive and
emotional and always cries to her mom. I never want
to make it worse but she is driving me crazy. She's
obsessed with this Hannah Fletch bat mitzvah thing
and always asking everyone so many questions about
it. I mean, we're not invited, so can she just try and
get over it or at least put it out of her mind? Why
is she torturing herself with these questions and at
the same time torturing me, too? IT'S MAKING ME
SO CRAZY!!!!!!!!!!!! Also, I don't think I want to spend
the summer with her and Mara and Mae. It was fine
when it was just Mara and me but now I feel like Mae
is nervous about it and I just want to go and feel free

and not be so bogged down by all of these people and their stress. I need to get out of it. My gut is saying get out of it but I don't even know how. I don't want to hurt anyone's feelings. I just want to not feel so stressed. UGH. Please help.

Love, Cecily

Pri! Did we discuss the poem in your pocket idea? We need to pass that along as well. I think it would be so cute.

Sage! How does it work?

Basically everyone brings in little slips of paper with poems on them and then they pass them to people in the hallway and they put them in their pockets and then pass and on and on . . .

Isn't this like the take a poem, leave a poem thing? The one we are doing with the bowls?

Kinda but poem in your pocket just sounds so cute, doesn't it?

Yeah, we can add it. I feel like we can just do as much as possible with poetry for the full month.

Agree

Hiii Journal!!

So for the first time in forever I feel like things are actually fine with my friends. I am in a good place with Ivy and in a good place with my school friends, even Miriam and stuff. And I am soooo excited I was invited to Hannah F's bat mitzvah. But this school thing is insane. What am I gonna do? I may need to go to summer school for real and then what about Outdoor Explorers? Why is everything so hard all of a sudden? I should probably stop writing here and get to work but I can't focus. It's kind of making me crazy.

Okay, bye.
Love, Gabs

BLENDED

Wonder

SMILE

A Crooked Kind of Perfect

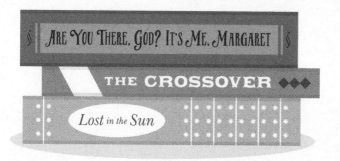

ARE YOU THERE, GOD? IT'S ME, MARGARET

THE CROSSOVER

Lost in the Sun

Cassie Was Here

OUT OF MY MIND

HARBOR ME

Miriam, Gabrielle

MIRIAM

Hi

GABRIELLE

Hiiiiii

MIRIAM

What are u up to

GABRIELLE

Trying to do hw

U

MIRIAM

Same

But I wanted to ask u something

Is Cece ok

MIRIAM

I felt really bad about her crying @ lunch

GABRIELLE

IK

I feel like she is prob fine

She holds everything in

And then bursts at random times

MIRIAM

Oh

GABRIELLE

I mean obv she wishes she was invited

But Cece is strong

And a genius

She will be ok

MIRIAM

Yeah

MIRIAM

I feel so bad but I am just sooooo excited

GABRIELLE

I know

Me too

Did I tell u Pri & I & our moms are going shopping together

MIRIAM

Yeah

My mom said I can get a new dress, too

GABRIELLE

Ooh so fun

MIRIAM

Ya

K just wanted to say hi & check in

GABRIELLE

Cool

GABRIELLE

Back to hw

MIRIAM

If u ever want to meet for another hw date I am totally game

GABRIELLE

Thanx maybe

Bye

MIRIAM

Bye

Prianka, Gabrielle

PRIANKA

Sooooo excited for our shopping day

Did u tell the other girls we're going

GABRIELLE

No

You?

PRIANKA

No

Don't want to rub anything in

GABRIELLE

Same ✓✓✓

PRIANKA

But what if they ask us for plans

GABRIELLE

IDK

We'll say we are busy with diff stuff

Did I tell u my mom and I have a meeting with Ms. Brickfeld in guidance about summer school

PRIANKA

Noooo

But what about outdoor explorers

GABRIELLE

IDK

May shorten the time

I feel like I need extra help tho

And I may get tested for ADD or ADHD or both

PRIANKA

For real

This feels like so much to deal with, Gabs

I'm sorry

GABRIELLE

It is too much 😭😭😭

But may explain why school has always been hard

And why it's so hard for me now

PRIANKA

Yeah could be good

GABRIELLE

Maybe I could have been in honors all along LOL 👩👩📚

PRIANKA

Who even cares about honors tho

GABRIELLE

Yeah

But it's a thing

And people take it seriously

PRIANKA

Yeah but

It doesn't measure your self worth

I don't believe in it YKWIM

We are more than grades

GABRIELLE

Haha ok, Pri

U r seeming really intense rn

PRIANKA

It's how I feel

We need to dig deeper

GABRIELLE

Ok

Rn I need to dig deeper into my hw

PRIANKA

LOL k

GABRIELLE

Bye 😘

PRIANKA

Bye 😘

From: Evelyn Brickfeld
To: Gabrielle Katz, Diana Katz
Subject: Summer

Dear Gabby and Diana,

Wonderful to meet with both of you! I've spoken to all of Gabby's teachers. We're in the process of lining up some weekly after-school extra help sessions for her as well. I'm also going to recommend an evaluation to rule out ADD or ADHD. Our school psychologist, Ms. Arlo, can help with that.

Please be in touch with any questions.

All my very best wishes,
Evelyn

FRIENDS

GABRIELLE

Hi, guys

I have to tell u something

Anyone there

Helloooooo

Ok bye

Dear Mom, I'm happy you suggested this. It's a little weird but I'm willing to give it a try. You asked if I have anything on my mind and I actually do. I hope you won't be mad, though. Here goes... I don't want to do the summer volunteer corps thing. It seemed great but I just don't want to. I feel tied down with Mara and Mae and Victoria and I want to be on my own. I always feel like I am responsible for people and I don't want to be. I wrote to the program and it's okay to cancel. Thanks in advance for understanding. Love, Cecily

Oh, Cecily, wow. I am sorry to hear this. You should never feel locked into anything like this, especially at your age. That said, commitments are important. I think we need to sort out why you don't want to do it, and see if there is any way to get around it. Maybe summer can be a combination of programs. I know this is our first journal exchange, but this seems like something better discussed face-to-face. I love you.

FRIENDS

VICTORIA

Hi, guys

Sorry I wasn't around before

How is everyone ? ?

GABRIELLE

Hi

I am ok

I need to tell u guys something

I'm being tested for ADD

VICTORIA

Really 👀 👀

GABRIELLE

Yeah

GABRIELLE

Might explain a lot of my issues all along with school

VICTORIA

Wow 😵 😵 😵 😵

R u ok

GABRIELLE

I am

I think

A little nervous for the eval

PRIANKA

We are here for u, Gabs

CECILY

Definitely

& since we are confessing things

GABRIELLE

Well this isn't really a confession but

CECILY

Vic, this mostly pertains to you

VICTORIA

Uh-oh

CECILY

I think I may drop out of volunteer corp

My heart isn't in it

I want to do something totally on my own this summer

VICTORIA

Omg, Cece

CECILY

I love u

U know that

VICTORIA

Can we pls discuss in person tho

CECILY

We can

GABRIELLE

Way to steal my moment, Cece

CECILY

LOL

GABRIELLE

Not laughing

Whatever I gtg

PRIANKA

Guys WIGO 😵😵😵😲😐😲

VICTORIA

Things just went from calm 2 crazy in 2 min
😵😵😵

PRIANKA

For real 🙃🙃🙃

VICTORIA

Things always feel on the verge of insanity

PRIANKA

TBH, IKWYM

Cecily has left the chat

Gabrielle has left the chat

VICTORIA

Ugghhhhhshshshsh

PRIANKA

For real, Vic

Mara, Cecily

MARA

Victoria just texted me

What is this about u not coming to the summer program

CECILY

I just feel suffocated

I want to do my own thing

MARA

But u made a commitment

CECILY

I know

And I feel really bad

But it just doesn't feel right to me

MARA

I don't even know what to say

Is this bc of Mae coming

CECILY

No

Honestly I just want to be on my own

MARA

No matter what program u do, u won't be on your own

I can't talk about this anymore

I am so angry

CECILY

I'm sorry

To: Summer in Maine Volunteer Corps Staff
From: Cecily Anderson
Subject: Decision

Dear Ms. Tolaf:

I will not be attending the Summer in Maine Volunteer Corps program. Many thanks for understanding.

Sincerely,
Cecily Anderson

I'm not afraid of storms, for I'm learning how to sail my ship.
—Louisa May Alcott

From: Mr. Akiyama
To: Yorkville Middle School Students
Subject: Poem in Your Pocket Day

Hi, students,

See below for an email from Prianka Basak and Sage Zelnick

Hiiii, fellow students,

We are SO excited Poetry Month is here! And guess what? We are officially declaring Friday as Poem in Your Pocket Day! It's an annual NYC thing and we're bringing it to Yorkville Middle School!

So here's what you have to do: make copies or write out your favorite poem on slips of paper and put them in your pocket and carry them around all day! Share them as many times as you can: with fellow students and teachers and people on the street. Anyone, really! There will also be a mic set up in the auditorium, so pop in and read your poem aloud.

Yay!!! Enjoy Yorkville Middle School's first annual POEM IN YOUR POCKET DAY!

Yours in poetry,
Prianka Basak & Sage Zelnick

Prianka, Cecily

P C

PRIANKA

Cece?

I wanted to reach out & check in and make sure u r ok   🖤🖤🖤🖤🖤🖤🖤🖤
😍😘

U don't seem like urself lately 😟 😟

CECILY

I am ok

I feel better actually

A weight off my shoulders

I may do this program where we help rebuild homes in El Salvador

It's late to apply but if I get a scholarship I can go

My parents can't afford all these fancy things the kids do here

People don't understand that not everyone is rich

And I just feel like I need some space from it all

PRIANKA

Yeah I know what you mean

That's sorta how Gabs felt earlier this year with the different groups

CECILY

I know but that's not how I feel

I just want to literally be on my own

And do my own thing

With nobody I know

PRIANKA

Wow, Cece

That feels super intense

CECILY

I know

It's the truth tho

Gotta explore

Be free

I feel burnt out TBH

PRIANKA

Got it

Glad u understand

I don't feel the same

But I know what you mean

That counts, too

LOL k

Mwah

Mwah

Prianka, Vishal

VISHAL

Yo

PRIANKA

Hey

VISHAL

This poetry stuff is cool

PRIANKA

Duh I know

VISHAL

I didn't realize it before

YKWIM

PRIANKA

Yeah well glad u like it

VISHAL

Good job, Pri

PRIANKA

Lol thanks

Hiiiiiii

C P G V

VICTORIA

Hi, guys

Putting all the   aside

I had an idea 💡💡💡💡💡

Anyone there ⁉️

Hiiiiiii

C P G V

CECILY

Hi sorry

What's ur idea

VICTORIA

I think we should plan a pool day and
sleepover just the 4 of us before we all part
ways for summer

Not to be exclusive but just keep it chill

We r always so happy @ the pool

Wouldn't that be so fun

CECILY

Ya

GABRIELLE

This could be great 👊🏻👊🏻

PRIANKA

Hiiii 👋🏾👋🏾👋🏾

Sorry just seeing this

I was knee deep in poetry month stuff

CECILY

How is that going

PRIANKA

So great ✅✅✅

What did u guys think of poem in your pocket day 🤗🤗🤗

VICTORIA

I loved it 🖤🖤🖤

And everyone was so into the Shel Silverstein one I brought in

VICTORIA

Not everyone knew it

PRIANKA

So cool 😎 🎉 🎊

CECILY

I gtg but I luv the pool day idea

GABRIELLE

I'll help plan it with u, Vic

After all the craziness lately I feel like I need something chill

VICTORIA

Sounds great

PRIANKA

Bye, guys 👋 👋 👋

Get excited to write poems in sidewalk chalk tomorrow!!!!!!!!!

Cecily, Mara

CECILY

Hi

Can u talk

I feel like you're ignoring me

I'd love to chat with you

Dear Mara,

First of all, I want to apologize. What I did wasn't right. I know I made a commitment and I know I let you down. I know all of that. I'm not saying it's right. I'm just saying it was something I needed to do. I feel like sometimes in life we have to make choices, and they're not always the popular ones. And that's what happened to me in this case. I just had this anxious feeling that this summer program wasn't the right thing. I kept trying to convince myself that it would be okay but ultimately I had a terrible feeling about it. I'm so sorry. You have a right to be mad at me but I just wish we could talk about it. Is there any chance you'll discuss it with me? We could go for a walk if that makes it easier. That's really all I ask. Please hear me out.

Love, Cecily

Just had a brainstorm. What if we started a poetry camp for the elementary school kids? Wouldn't that be awesome?! Prob can't do it for this summer, but for next summer...

Really? Could we do that?

I think we could! Let's talk to someone. I feel like I eat, sleep, breathe poetry! Also I just want to start things & make a difference & heal the world! HEAL THE WORLD THROUGH POETRY!! :) :)

I love it!

Prianka, Gabrielle

P G

Sooooo excited for shopping day today

I really want something sparkly

Do u have any idea what u want

GABRIELLE

Hmmm 🤔🤔🤔

Tbh I have been too stressed to think about it 😱😨😱

This whole thing with the ADD evaluation 🙁☹️😣

I haven't told many people about it but I am overwhelmed 😬😬😬

201

Oh, Gabs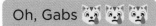

What can I do to help u

GABRIELLE

IDK 😥😥😢😢😢😓😥

But thank u

See u soon 👋🏻👋🏻

Cecily,

Thanks for your note. I'm still really disappointed but I understand that you had to make this decision even if I don't like it at all. Don't worry—our friendship isn't over. And we'll always be neighbors anyway. :)

Well, until college. :)

Love, Mara

Dear Journal,

I'm about to go shopping with Prianka and
moms and I just can't believe the timing of this
evaluation. I guess I was happier when I didn't
know the results or didn't have the results. Now
that I do know them, I feel all weird. I have ADD
but it's sometimes called ADHD. The kind I have
isn't so hyper though. It's confusing, this disorder.
It's why I often feel like I can't focus and things
are all over the place. I zone out when people
talk and I have trouble paying attention in class. I
guess it's good to know, but it's also scary. What
can I even do with this information? I just want
to go shopping and find a fun dress for Hannah's
bat mitzvah but I can't even be excited about that.
There's too much stress surrounding the event
anyway and now this. UGH. I just want to get
back into bed and bury my head under the pillow.

Love, Gabs

Prianka, Gabrielle

Omg my mom is vetoing every dress

GABRIELLE

Haha yeah why is she so stressed

PRIANKA

IDK

She hates when there is too much exposed skin

GABRIELLE

LOL 😜😜

I think my mom just wants to find something here and go home

Is ur mom in the dressing room w/ u

No outside

Yours

Yes

Ugh

She looks annoyed

I wish we could've gone shopping on our own 😬😬😬

Same

Ok put down phone & try on & come show me & I'll do the same

K

Prianka, Gabrielle

PRIANKA

TBH I'm glad that experience is behind us

Omg Mama Basak

GABRIELLE

Haha same

PRIANKA

I'm happy with the dress but I just wanted 2 be done

GABRIELLE

Haha same (again)

PRIANKA

Talk later, Gabs Love u ♥♥♥

GABRIELLE

Mwah

Hi, Mom,

I couldn't find our mom/daughter journal but
this piece of paper is just as good. I wondered if
you and Dad have given any more thought to the
El Salvador program. The more I think about it,
the more I want to do it. I really feel a need to
be on my own. If I get in, it's all free of
charge. Let me know if I should apply.
It's really late but they told me when
I called there's still time to apply
for a scholarship.

Love, Cecily

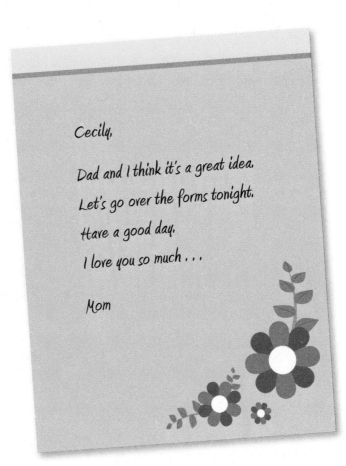

Cecily,

Dad and I think it's a great idea.
Let's go over the forms tonight.
Have a good day.
I love you so much . . .

Mom

Dear Mara,

I know I hurt you and I want to apologize for letting you down. Deep in my heart, I truly feel that I am making the right decision. However, I know I broke a promise to you and that makes me feel terrible. Please know how sorry I am.

Love, Cecily

Dear Vic,

We've had our ups and downs but I know I really feel we've had more ups than downs, and for that reason, I am so sorry I upset you about the summer trip. I just had to do something different and I hope you understand. You can be angry at me, I get it. I just want you to know I am truly sorry.

Love, Cece

Cece!

I totally get it. Honestly. TBH, I'm okay
with it, too. Mara, Mae & I are still
going & Mae and I have gotten super
close over text. I feel like it's okay. For
the first time in forever I honestly feel
okay. I am not even that sad about the
bat mitzvah thing anymore. I have made
peace with it. I am excited about the
summer plans. I feel good. So please
don't worry. K?

Love, VM

From: Prianka Basak
To: Gabrielle Katz, Victoria Melford, Cecily Anderson
Subject: RE: MY HOUSE AFTER SCHOOL

Hi! I'm replying for all of us since we're all in comp lab right now. WE WILL BE THERE!!!!!!!!!!!!!!!!!!!!

LOVE FOREVS!
Pri

> **From:** Cecily Anderson
> **To:** Prianka Basak, Gabrielle Katz, Victoria Melford
> **Subject:** MY HOUSE AFTER SCHOOL
>
> Hi, guys—
>
> I am just sitting here in study hall and realizing that there is a major disconnect going on. We're all bogged down. But let's de-bog ourselves! I want to have a quality hang sesh at my house after school. Just come, we'll do homework

and snack and talk and chill and RECONNECT. OKAY? I know you're all free today so don't make up an excuse. We can't wait for the pool day to really bond. WE NEED TO DO IT NOW.

XOXO Cece

Ivy, Gabrielle

IVY

Are u coming to the reunion

I didn't see u on the RSVP list

GABRIELLE

No I can't make it

I feel too overwhelmed

GABRIELLE

Plus there's a big bat mitzvah here that day and I need to get ready 👗

It's really fancccyyyyyy

IVY

Oh

I'll miss u 😟😟😟😟

GABRIELLE

Same 🐱😿

But I'll see u sooooo sooooon 🎉🎉🎉

And guess what

I can do summer school at the end of the summer & still come to first session of camp 🐧🐧

My parents discussed it and they don't want me to miss all of camp 🏕️🏕️🏕️🌲🌳

IVY

OMG that is such great news 👊👊

GABRIELLE

IK 🙌🙏🙌👧👩👩

I am so happy
😑😑😑😑😑😑😑😑😑😑😑😑

IVY

We are going to have the best time
🎉🎊🎉🎊🎉🎊

Still wish u were coming to the reunion tho
😭

IK same

But why do we need a reunion so close to summer 💁💁

IVY

Good point

I guess they want everyone to get excited about it 🎉🎉🎉

GABRIELLE

Prob yeah

Makes sense

IVY

Do u want me to spy on Eli for u

GABRIELLE

Hahahah what

IVY

Ya know

GABRIELLE

No not really

IVY

To see if he says anything about u

GABRIELLE

Oh haha

That's not really spying

IVY

U know what I mean 🙄🙄

GABRIELLE

Yeah but no thanx

I'm good

IVY

U don't like him

GABRIELLE

IDK

Too stressed to focus on boys rn

IVY

K

Love u, Gabs 🤍🖤🤍💖

GABRIELLE

Love u 2 😍😍😍😍

Hi, guys. So I know we're doing another one of these sit in a circle and write to each other things but it's very important. Do you see why? Have any of you noticed something significant going on with this notebook?

Ummmm??? Cleary Pri is just as oblivious here as I am, Cece! jk, Pri!
XOXOX Gabs

Um, same here, Pri. Confused Victoria as usual...

Guys! We only have a few pages left! We are finishing this notebook...like, today, probably!!! We need to finish it off on the right foot, or, um, page or whatever. LOL

So what should we do??

Confess our undying love for each other, obviously. DUH!

Maybe we each write a reflection on life and the notebook and how we've changed since we started it?

Um, yeah, for real. I mean, I wasn't even part of it when you guys started it. This notebook has been kinda life changing for me.

LOL, drama queen Vic. But okay. All good ideas.

You go first, Cece. Since you're the only who noticed we're nearing the very end of this beautiful collection of paper.

So poetic, Pri. Obv you need to write a poem for your reflection.

Got it. Will do.

I can't be the one to start. I'm feeling too emotional over here.

I'll do it. But give me a few minutes to collect my thoughts. Talk amongst yourselves.
Hahahahahahahaha

Pri's Reflections

Isn't it strange how you can find a notebook
   at a store
And it can turn into anything at all
This notebook could have been something
   so boring
Used for taking notes in class
Or a plumber writing down what plumbing work
   he had to do

Or a person writing grocery lists

Or who even knows what

But when Cece got this notebook

It became something magical

All of these thoughts and conversations

All of our feelings

Right there on the page

I'm so glad this notebook is ours

Such a simple thing really

And yet it connected us to one another

Do we start another one?

That's what I want to know.

I have to say that I feel like a completely different person from when we started this notebook. The ADHD diagnosis feels like a really big deal. I never knew I was struggling with a real thing. I just thought I was easily distracted. I want to thank you guys for being so supportive and amazing. For standing by me when I wasn't the best version of myself or the best friend to all of you. I am really grateful. I love you guys. Thank you for giving me the space to make new friends while also welcoming me back.

First of all, can we please discuss how much I have evolved? I didn't even really freak when Cece changed her summer plans. And I got over the Hannah F bat mitzvah sadness really fast. I kind of think I evolved and changed the most out of all of us. I don't want to start a fight or anything but think about it. You may agree with me?

Okay, not having a debate about who has changed the most. We all have, duh. Also, did you guys know people change the most in the three years of middle school more than any other time in their lives (except for newborn babies to two years old)? Crazy, right?

Very crazy, Pri. Love all of your scientific knowledge.

So what do we do with that info? Where does that leave us?

Very deep, Cece. Here's the deal, guys. I've narrowed it down. We can change all we want and our friendships will, too, but the heart and soul of it all will remain the same

You should read that at the poetry jam, Gabs!!!!

Ooooh, maybe I will!

Here's how I break it down: We may be apart this summer and apart in some classes and apart during various times in our lives, and we may feel distant from each other when things like Hannah F's bat mitzvah come around. And the thing is, eventually we'll be apart more than we're together. But here's the deal (and I think one of you told me this but I don't remember who, sorry)...

TBH, we're always gonna be apart but still together.

Forever and ever and ever...

GLOSSARY

2 to

2gether together

2morrow tomorrow

4 for

4eva forever

4get forget

any1 anyone

awk awkward

bc because

BFF best friends forever

BFFAE best friends forever and ever

BI Block Island

BNF best neighbors forever

b-room bathroom

b/t between

c see

caf cafeteria

comm committee

COMO crying over missing out

comp computer

deets details

def definitely

DEK don't even know

diff different

disc discussion

emo emotional

every1 everyone

fab fabulous

fabolicious extra fabulous

fac faculty

fave favorite

Fla Florida

FOMO fear of missing out

fone phone

FYI for your information

gd god

gg gotta go

gma grandma

gn good night

gnight good night

gr8 great

gtg got to go

hw homework

ICB I can't believe

IDC I don't care

IDEK I don't even know

IDK I don't know

IHNC I have no clue

IK I know

IKWYM I know what you mean

ILY I love you

ILYSM I love you so much

JK just kidding

K OK

KIA know-it-all

KWIM know what I mean

l8r later

LMK let me know

LOL laugh out loud

luv love

n e way anyway

NM nothing much

nums numbers

nvm never mind

obv obviously

obvi obviously

obvs obviously

OMG oh my God

ooc out of control

PBFF poetry best friend forever

peeps people

perf perfect

pgs pages

plzzzz please

pos possibly

q question

r are/our

ridic ridiculous

rlly really

RN right now

sci science

sec second

sem semester

scheds schedules

shud should

some1 someone

SWAK sealed with a kiss

TBH to be honest

thx thanks

tm tomorrow

TMI too much information

tmrw tomorrow

tomrw tomorrow

tomw tomorrow

totes totally

ttyl talk to you later

u you

ur your; you're

urself yourself

vv very, very

w/ with

wb write back

whatev whatever

WIGO what is going on

wknd weekend

w/o without

WTH what the heck

wud would

wut what

wuzzzz what's

Y why

ACKNOWLEDGMENTS

& to my incredible editor, Maria Barbo, who believed in the TBH from the beginning. I cannot ever thank you enough! for Alyssa Eisner Henkin, dream agent who has been by my side for close to 13 years. for Alice @ Trident and for the fabulous KT books team: Katherine, Stephanie, Camille, Liz, Mark, Molly, Amy, Kristen, Sam, & Vaishali. for my BWL crew, my loves Dave, Aleah, and Hazel and of course all of the TBH fans. Keep reading!!! xoxoxoxox

LISA GREENWALD lives in NYC 🍎 w/ her husband & 2 young daughters 👨👩👧👧. She ❤️s: 😎 📚 🏖️ & 🧁. Summer is her favorite season ☀️ 🌞 🍉 🍨 🍦 🏖️ 🕶️. Visit her 💻 @ www.lisagreenwald.com.

Great books by
LISA GREENWALD!

The Friendship List

TBH